KING LION AND HIS COOKS

First published in the United States in 1982 by Holt, Rinehart
and Winston, 383 Madison Avenue, New York, New York 10017.

Library of Congress Cataloging in Publication Data
Brierley, Louise.
King Lion and his cooks.
Summary: King Lion has a different cook for each day
Monday through Friday, but on the weekend he must take
matters into his own hands.
[1. Lions—Fiction.   2. Kings, queens, rulers, etc.—
Fiction.   3. Cookery—Fiction]   I. Title.
PZ7.B7642Ki   1982   [Fic] __ 81-17132
ISBN 0-03-061218-7   AACR2

First American Edition
Printed in Italy
1 3 5 7 9 10 8 6 4 2

KING LION
AND HIS COOKS

LOUISE BRIERLEY

HOLT, RINEHART AND WINSTON   NEW YORK

Long ago King Lion ruled the land. He was a very handsome king and had all the kingly virtues. He was wise and brave and generous. His only fault was that he ate too much. He loved food more than everything else in his kingdom. He even removed all the fine old paintings from the royal art gallery and in their place put pictures of his five royal cooks. When foreign visitors came to court, the king would take them to the gallery and tell them tales of his five cooks and their five delicious dishes.

 The first of these cooks, Mademoiselle Mouse, was chosen for her excellent cheese soufflé. Every Monday she would drag her light, fluffy soufflé from her kitchen behind the molding to the royal table.

Mistress Cow was chosen for her rich creamy milk. Every Tuesday she would give the smoothest milk in the land, put it in a large churn, and send it up to the palace.

 Master Cat was chosen because he caught the finest fish in the sea. Every Wednesday he delivered a platter of the fattest fish, the reddest lobsters, and the juiciest shrimps to the royal table.

 Mister Toad was chosen for his very special creation of smooth batter and spicy sausages known as toad-in-the hole. Every Thursday he took up his oars to row the mouth-watering dish from his riverside home to the palace gate.

Mistress Goose was chosen because she laid the finest eggs in the land. Every Friday she would dress in her best bonnet and apron and, with a curtsy, deliver her nicest egg, decorated in crimson and gold, to King Lion.

But on weekends King Lion had
no special cook. His breakfast was
leftovers. His dinner was leftovers.
And he was bored. One Saturday he decided it just
was not good enough. The food set before him
was not fit for a king. Another dish must be
prepared. He would himself go to the royal library
and find a new recipe.

He hurried down royal corridors, up royal stairs, along royal passages, and through at least a hundred royal doors until he reached the library. There were books on every subject. Books on art, books on music, and books on dancing. Books on mathematics, books on astronomy, and books on engineering. Books in English, books in French, and books in Latin. Books which had pictures and books which had none. And at last, in one of the dullest books with almost no pictures at all, the king found the recipe he wanted.

"Broth!" he shouted. "That's it. My five cooks will make me a good plain broth. On weekends I will eat broth."

King Lion ran back through royal corridors and passages, down royal stairs, and through at least a hundred royal doors to the council chamber. The five cooks were summoned. "On Saturday you will make broth," he declared.

The next Saturday the five cooks gathered around the big kettle in the kitchen. Mistress Cow poured in milk, adding a little too much so that milk would be the strongest flavor. Master Cat threw in fish and then secretly a lobster to make sure his was the strongest taste. Mademoiselle Mouse stirred in cheese, adding a little extra because she knew the king would like cheese best. Dame Goose put in an egg and then, when no one was looking, added another. And Mister Toad threw in one sausage and followed it with a whole string.

The great moment came for the broth to be served. In the royal dining room the king sat down to eat. He raised the spoon to his lips. The five cooks watched eagerly. They waited for the words, "This is the finest broth in the world!"

But instead the king let out a great roar. "It's aargh—horrible! It's too fishy! It's too cheesy! It's too milky! There's too much sausage! The eggs taste vile. I will not eat it." And in a rage King Lion kicked over the table and chair, scattering the frightened cooks in all directions.

For a week the cooks were too frightened to come to court. The king was in a towering rage. He was too angry even to speak to anybody. His kingdom fell into chaos.

But you will remember that King Lion was a wise king. At the end of the week, he summoned his five cooks to court. "We were very angry when you served broth not fit for a king," he began (for kings always say "we" when they are feeling important). "We did not eat for a week and we ignored the affairs of the kingdom. But, if a king is to govern wisely, he must think of more than his stomach. You are all good cooks and on five days of the week we will honor you as such. But on the other two, as a reminder that both cooks and kings can be wrong, we will make for ourselves a simple broth. And let it be proclaimed throughout the land that too many cooks spoil the broth!"